Dear Reader,

In the spring of 2007, a close family member was diagnosed with cancer. My husband and I talked through the best way to break the news to our children. We explained that cancer is a serious disease, but today many people are cured and many others live with cancer. What we didn't anticipate, and certainly weren't prepared for, were all the questions that followed.

"What is cancer?" my seven-year-old asked. That's a pretty straightforward question. Yet it never occurred to us, until that moment, that we had no idea what cancer was and why it happens. As we tried to answer, my eleven-year-old piped in with another question. Each time my husband and I responded, several more questions were raised.

Illness touches every family in one way or another. Is It Contagious? is committed to publishing books that convey complex information in both a creative and thoughtful manner. We hope our books will help dispel the mystery and fear surrounding many of the world's most common diseases.

Warmly,
Amy Koppelman, Founder

Copyright © 2009 by Vern Kousky. All rights reserved. Published in the United States by Is It Contagious? Books LLC, New York, New York. ISBN: 978-0-9824614-0-2

Is Cancer Contagious?

by Vern Kousky

Cancer is a disease we hear a lot about these days. Many of us know someone who has battled cancer. Some of us even have friends or family members who are right now fighting this disease. But what is cancer? Where does it come from?

Cancer is one of the most common diseases in the world. Almost every living creature can get it, from giraffes and birds...

...to even insects.

Cancer is so common because it comes from something all living things have in common. But what could this be?...

Think for a minute about your body. What is it made up of?

You may have thought of your hair and skin and bones. Or maybe you thought of organs, like your heart and lungs and brain. These are all good answers, but now try to think of what these parts are made up of.

Not sure? Well, just like something can be built out of Legos or building blocks, much of our bodies is built out of cells. Cells make up our skin, and cells make up our brains. In fact, the human body has more than 200 different kinds of cells. And each one of these has a special talent and an important job.

For example, our muscles are made up of special cells that can make themselves change size. Our bodies move by having many of these cells grow and shrink as a team.

Some parts of our bodies, however, are not made up of cells, but made by cells. Here we see bone-making cells building the hard parts of our bones.

You might be wondering why you can't see these cells,

...and that's because they are so tiny that we need a powerful microscope to see them.

Our cells are so tiny, in fact, that scientists think that we have as many as 100 trillion cells in our bodies.

To put it another way, if you counted one cell per second all day and all night, it would take you nearly 3 million years to count them all!

Now, we've mentioned that our cells are like building blocks or Legos in one way, but in another way they are very different. And that's because each and every cell is alive.

However, new cells are not created by being born the way people are born. When new cells are needed for our body, they make a copy of themselves by splitting in two. We call this mitosis.

There are several reasons why we need new cells. For many of you, your bodies are still growing, so lots of new cells must be created all the time. Also, since cells are alive, they eventually die. When this happens new cells must replace the old ones.

But cells don't always die just by wearing out. Whenever we hurt ourselves, what we really mean is that some of the cells in our bodies have died. And when we say that our cut or bruise is healing, this means our bodies are creating new cells to replace the damaged ones.

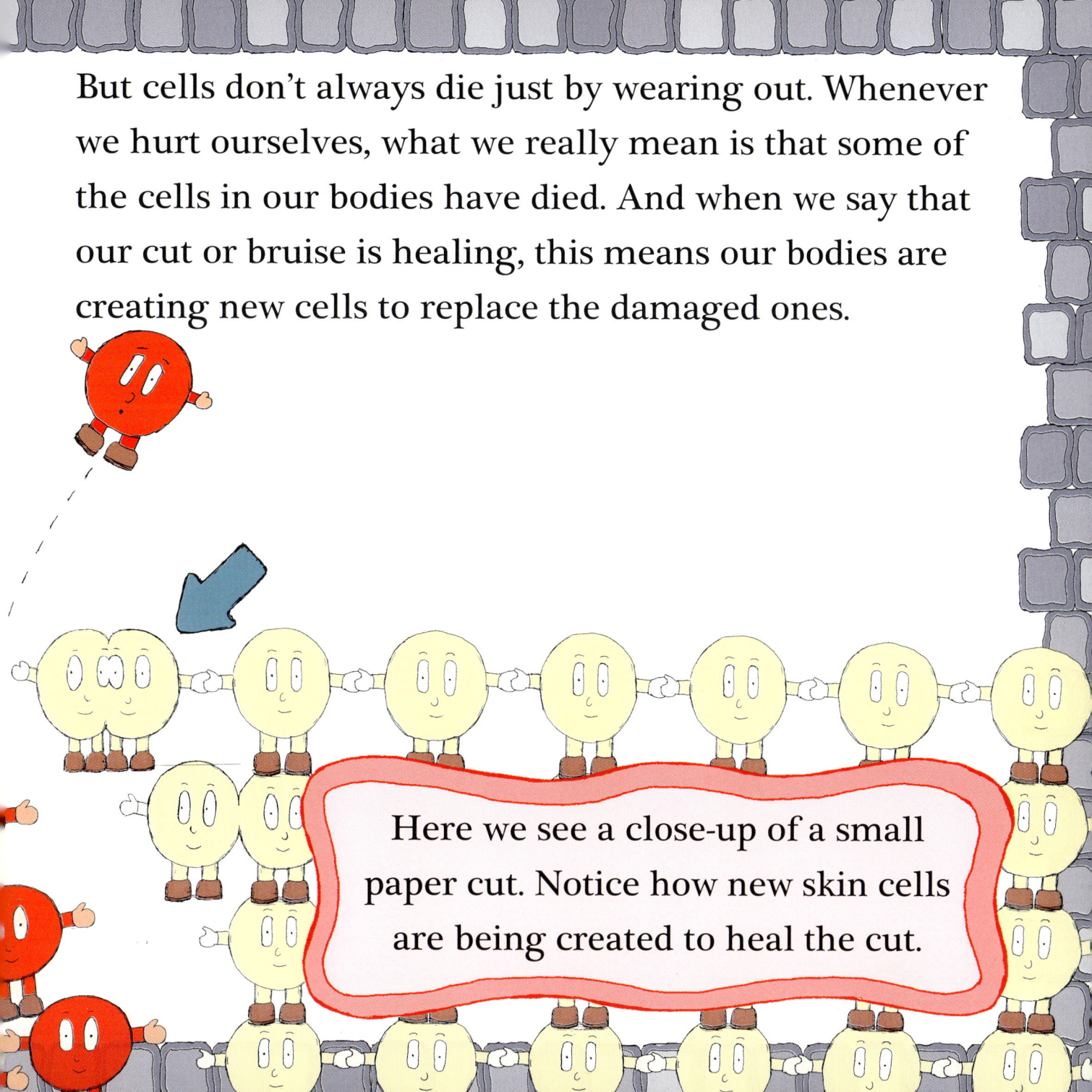

Here we see a close-up of a small paper cut. Notice how new skin cells are being created to heal the cut.

So what does all this have to do with cancer? Well, remember how we talked about how cells divide by mitosis to make copies of themselves?

Most of the time this works very well, but once in a while, the copy doesn't turn out just right. We call this mistake a mutation, and cancer comes from cell mutations.

Before we go on, it's important to understand that mutations aren't always a bad thing. To mutate really means to change. Most mutations are harmless, but they can be good as well as bad.

In fact, mutations allow plants and animals to change in ways that help them survive. Scientists think that changes like this are always happening, only very, very slowly. These changes, they think, are an important part of evolution. And evolution explains how, over millions of years, one type of animal can change into a completely different one.

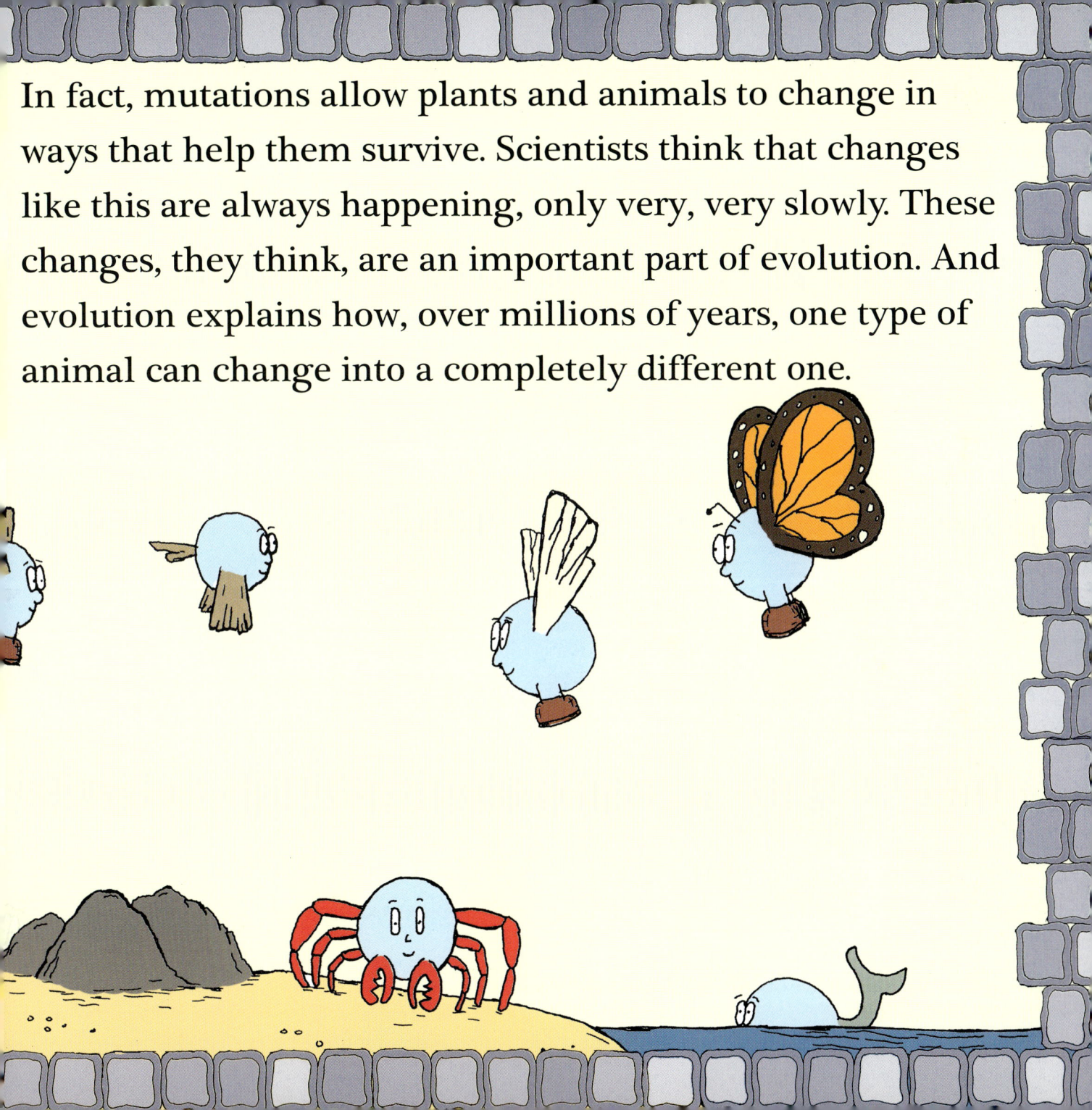

So how exactly can mutations cause cancer? Most of the time, our bodies find and get rid of these mutated cells. But once in a while, these cells stay alive and begin dividing very quickly. When this happens, they sometimes stick tightly together. The lump that they make is called a tumor.

Tumors like these usually stop soon after they begin growing and do not hurt normal cells. We call these tumors "benign," which means harmless. And while they are not always entirely harmless, they are usually easily removed.

But sometimes the tumors don't stop.

They keep growing...

...and growing.

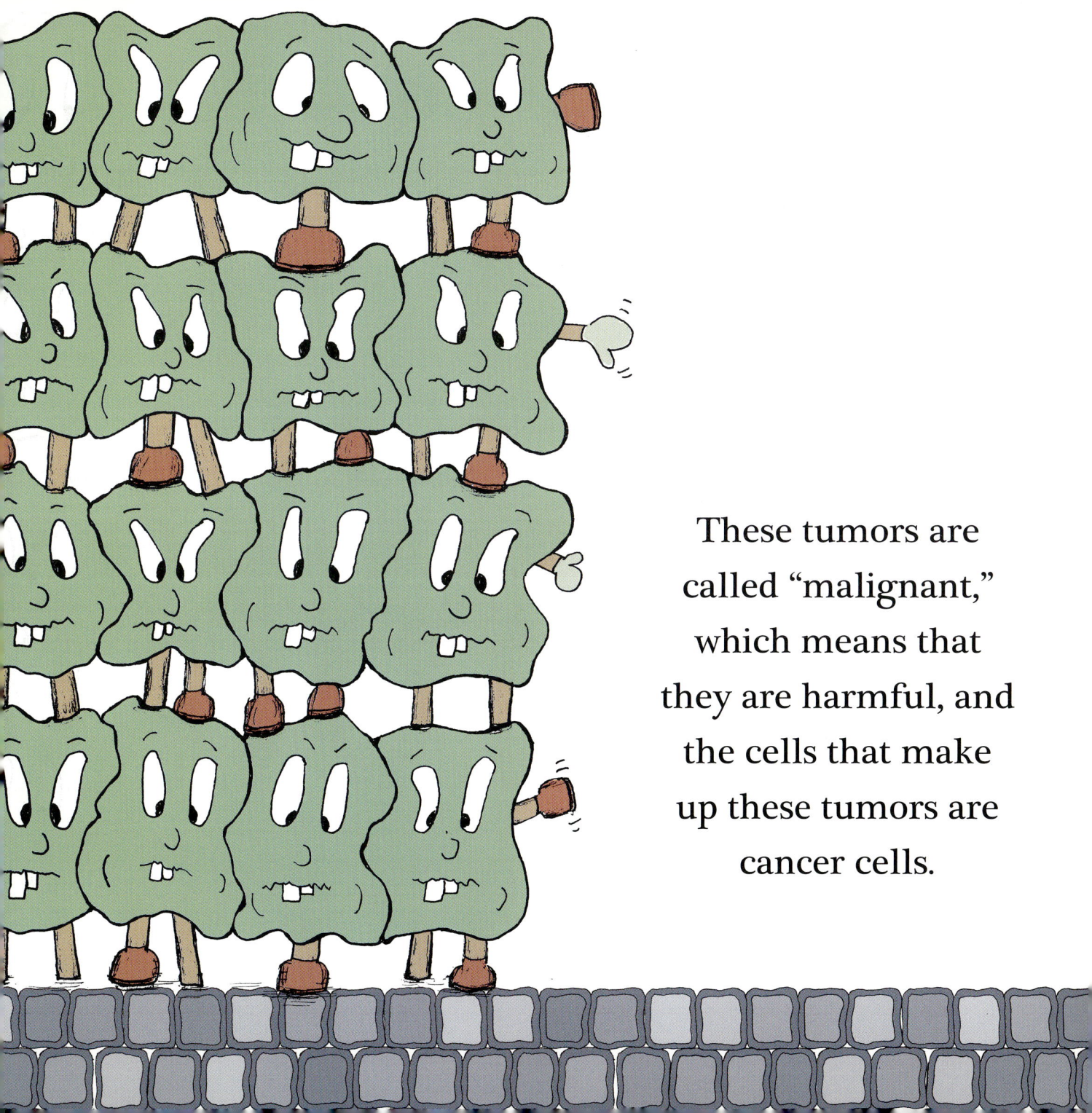

These tumors are called "malignant," which means that they are harmful, and the cells that make up these tumors are cancer cells.

But not all cancer cells stick together to make tumors. Cancer sometimes happens in the center of bones, which is called the bone marrow. The normal cells that live here are very important because they create new blood cells for our body.

Blood cells can also mutate into cancer. Blood cells perform a number of important jobs, like delivering oxygen and nutrients to different body parts. They also get rid of colds and stop the bleeding when we cut ourselves. Doctors call cancer of both blood and bone marrow "Leukemia."

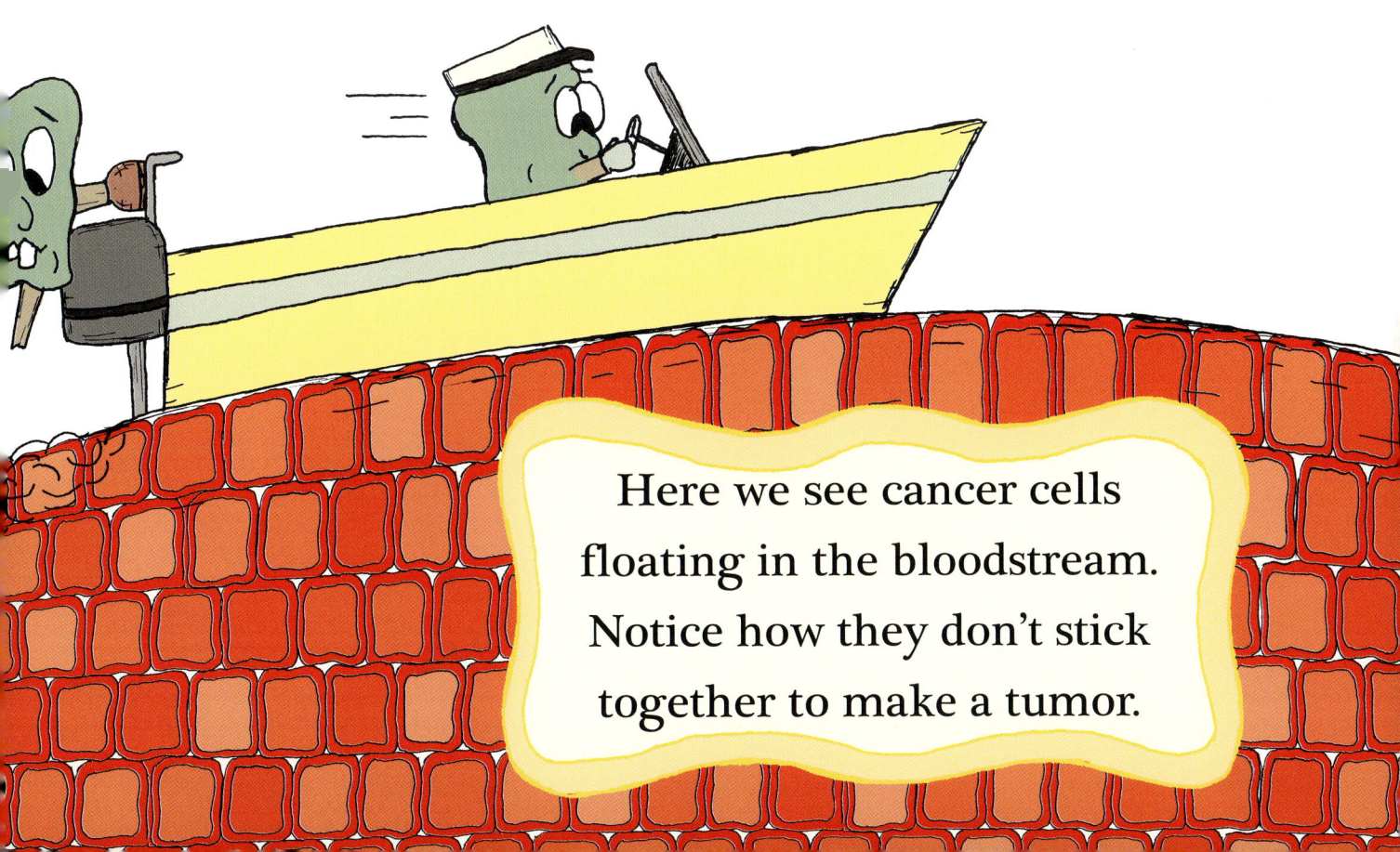

Here we see cancer cells floating in the bloodstream. Notice how they don't stick together to make a tumor.

Besides dividing like crazy and not doing their jobs, cancer cells do three other things:

First, cancer cells harm normal cells and keep them from doing their jobs.

Second, they don't die when they get old.

And third, they sometimes move to other parts of the body and begin dividing and growing all over again.

So how does cancer make people feel?

That's a tough one to answer. Since our bodies have over 200 different kinds of cells, there are over 200 different kinds of cancer. Sometimes cancer can make someone tired or not feel like eating. Sometimes cancer can make people feel just like they do when they have the flu or a cold. And sometimes there aren't any symptoms at first. Someone might feel bad only after the cancer spreads. This is why it is so important for everyone to see a doctor regularly. Doctors can sometimes spot cancer even when it doesn't make people feel sick.

But is cancer contagious?

You can't catch cancer the way you catch a cold. It's perfectly safe to hug someone who has cancer (And people with cancer like hugs just as much as you or I do!)

However, there are some things that make cell mutations more likely. And since cancer comes from cell mutations, these things make cancer more likely. We call these things "carcinogens."

So that we can stop cancer before it starts, let's take a look at two of the most common carcinogens that we can avoid....

Cigarettes and other tobacco products are the reason for nearly one out of every three cancers. This is because they contain many carcinogens and because so many people smoke all over the world.

However, sometimes people get cancer not by smoking themselves, but from spending a lot of time around people who smoke. This dangerous smoke is called "second-hand" smoke.

Another dangerous carcinogen is radiation. Radiation is invisible rays of energy that can harm or kill cells and make cancer more likely. Fortunately, most radiation is kept safely away from us, like the radiation from nuclear power. Or we don't get enough of it to harm us, like the radiation from X-rays. But there is one common type of radiation that we need to be careful of.

The sun sends out a type of radiation, called UV or ultra violet radiation. Most of you probably have felt this type of radiation. Whenever you get a sunburn, it is actually the sun's UV rays harming your cells. This is not cancer, and, like with X-rays, a short time in the sunshine is safe. But if you are going to spend a long time outside, it is very important to put sunblock on any parts of your skin your clothes do not protect. Sunblock helps block the sun's UV rays from harming you.

Now that we've learned some important things to avoid, let's look at two very important ways you can help prevent cancer.

First, you can eat healthy foods. Most fruits and vegetables are very good for us. They contain many vitamins and other nutrients to keep our bodies working well. Cereals made from grains like oats and wheat are good for us too (as long as they don't have lots of sugar). Fruits, vegetables and grains help make us healthy and strong, and healthy, strong bodies are better able to get rid of cancer cells.

Second, you can exercise regularly. Being overweight makes cancer more likely, and regular exercise is a good way to avoid being overweight.

But remember, exercise isn't only lifting weights or jogging.

Exercise can be riding a bike...

or playing a sport....

What happens when someone gets cancer?

Right now, there are several good ways to fight this disease. Let's take a look....

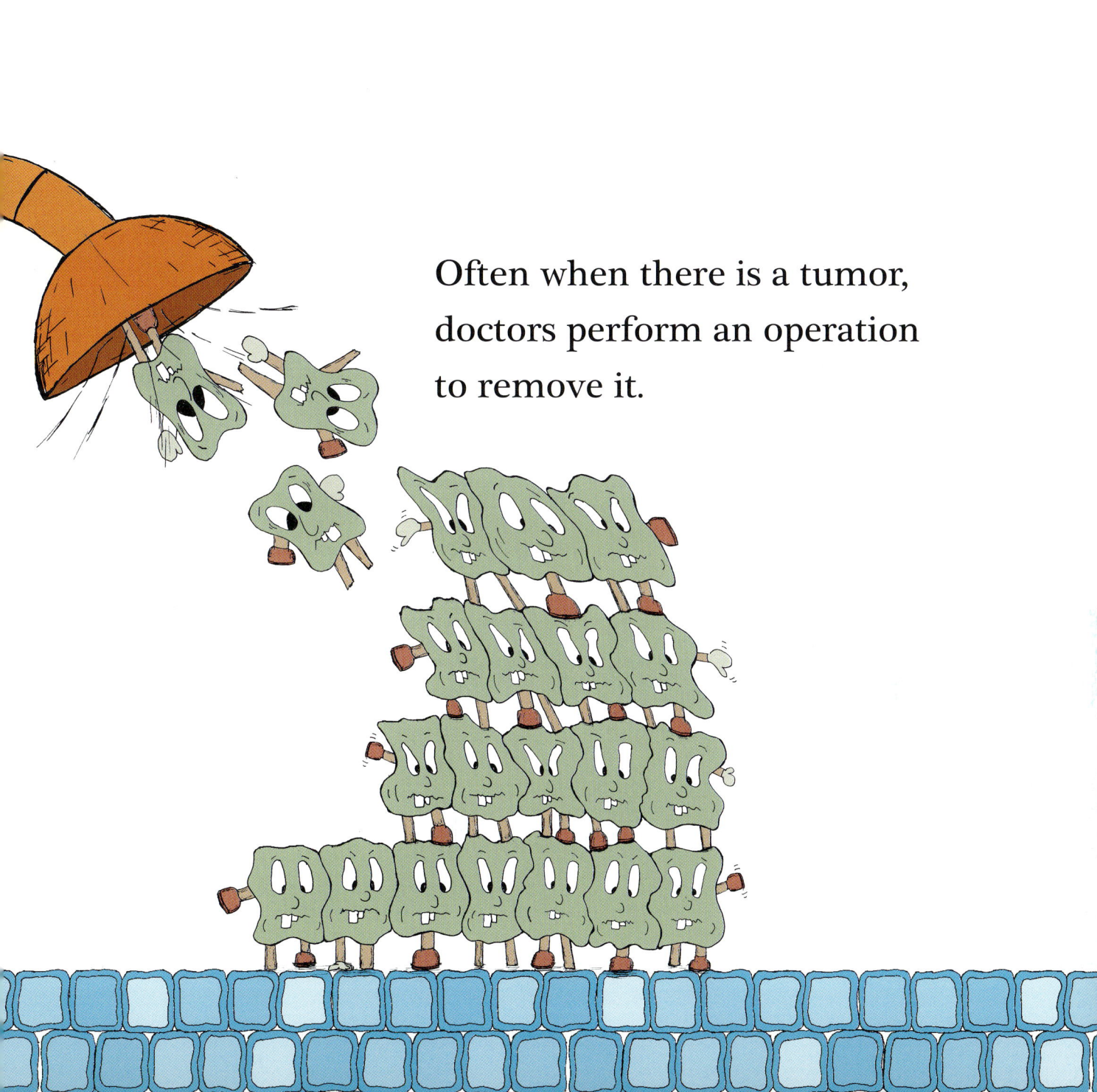

Often when there is a tumor, doctors perform an operation to remove it.

And then there's radiation. We've already learned how radiation can cause cancer, but radiation can also be used to fight cancer. With special machines, doctors can aim radiation at cancer cells to destroy them. This is called "radiation therapy" or "radiotherapy." Radiation therapy can destroy some tumors. Also, it is often used before an operation to shrink tumors or after an operation to stop the tumors from growing back.

Unfortunately, radiation therapy can harm some normal cells near the tumor, so people who have this done may feel tired, or lose their hair in certain places, or not feel like eating. We call these the "side effects" of treatment.

Like radiation therapy, chemotherapy destroys cancer cells. Chemotherapy is when chemical drugs are used that are specially made to only hurt quickly dividing cells like cancer cells.

Unfortunately, some normal cells also divide quickly. Blood cells, hair cells, and the cells that help us eat also divide this way and are harmed by chemotherapy. This is why people who have chemotherapy can have side effects like losing their hair, feeling tired, and feeling sick to their stomachs.

Even with all these treatments, scientists are still trying to find new ways to fight cancer. They are working to understand why cancer cells are different from normal cells and what makes them work.

One exciting possible treatment is called "targeted therapy." Once doctors target what makes the cancer cell strong they can make medicines that attacks a cancer cell's strength. Scientists are also looking at using antibodies. Antibodies are how our bodies fight sickness. Special antibodies are now being made that can help our bodies get rid of cancer cells without all the side effects of chemotherapy or radiation therapy.

Hopefully, this book has helped to make cancer a bit clearer for you. But if you ever have any questions, ask a teacher, a parent, or a doctor. They may not have all the answers either, but they can help you find where the answers are.

Also Available from Is It Contagious Books:

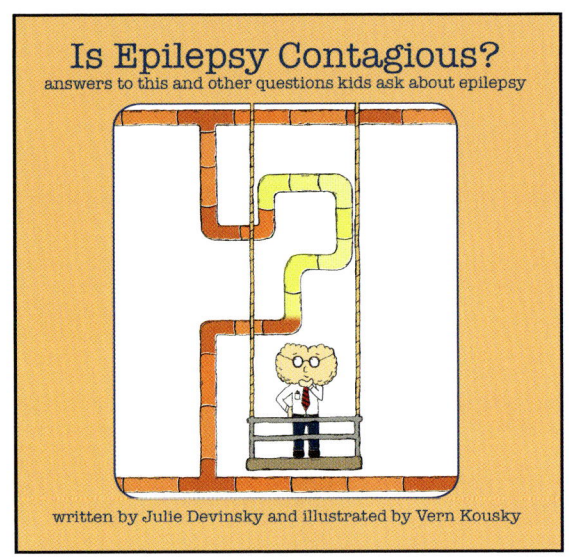

Coming soon:

- Is Heart Disease Contagious?
- Are Allergies and Asthma Contagious?

Please visit us on the web at isitcontagiousbooks.com for sales, additional resources, and information on upcoming titles.